Flip the book at this corner and see what I do with my boot.

A WORLD OF
SHOES

Written by
Della Rowland

Illustrated by FRANK RICCIO
Border Illustrations by SUMO

A CALICO BOOK
Published by Contemporary Books, Inc.
CHICAGO · NEW YORK

Library of Congress Cataloging-in-Publication Data
Rowland, Della.
A world of shoes / written by Della Rowland : illustrated by Frank
Riccio ; border illustrations by SUMO.
p.   cm.
"A Calico book."
Summary: Describes footwear worn by children from Japan, the
Soviet Union, Holland, England, and other countries.
ISBN 0-8092-4348-2
1. Shoes—Juvenile literature.   [1. Shoes.]   I. Riccio, Frank,
ill.   II. SUMO.   III. Title.
GT2130.R68   1989
391'.413'088054—dc19   88-35041
                                                    CIP
                                                    AC

Published by Contemporary Books, Inc.
180 North Michigan Avenue, Chicago, Illinois 60601
Manufactured in the United States of America
International Standard Book Number: 0-8092-4348-2

Published simultaneously in Canada by Beaverbooks, Ltd.
195 Allstate Parkway, Valleywood Business Park
Markham, Ontario L3R 4T8 Canada

Walk with me all around the world, and we shall see what shoes the children of different countries are wearing.

In Japan,
we wear wooden sandals
called geta (pronounced GET-ah).
They are like platforms
on little stilts.
Our geta
keep our feet dry
when it rains.
Sometimes
we wear socks called tabi (TAH-bee)
with our geta.

GETA—Japan

My boots were made for the saddle!
Their pointy toes slip right into the stirrups,
and the heels stop my feet from sliding forward.
The high tops aren't just for decoration.
They keep out the gravel my horse kicks up.

My boots aren't comfortable
for walking, though.
That's because, out West,
real cowboys and cowgirls
always ride!

BOOTS—Western United States

In the far,
far northern parts of Canada,
it is freezing cold.
But my feet stay warm
in my furry mukluks.
My mother
made them out of sealskin
to keep out the icy water
when I go fishing
with my father.

MUKLUKS—*Northern Canada*

My father makes babouches (bah-BOOSH)
and sells them in the marketplace.
He always has many customers.
Everyone in Morocco
wears these pointy slippers.
They are easy
to slip on and off
because they are all front
and no back!

BABOUCHES—Morocco

We invented rugby in England.
It's part soccer,
football, hockey, and basketball.

Rugby is a rough game.
Run! Push!
Our team has to fight hard
to score a goal.
Our leather rugby shoes
have cleats on the bottom,
so we can really dig in!

RUGBY SHOES—England

In Holland, we call our wooden clogs klompen.

Klomp! Klomp! Klomp!

Hear my clogs on the streets.

They are carved to fit my feet perfectly.

My best clogs are my favorites.

They're painted blue

and covered with red and yellow leather.

My brother says they are as pretty as tulips!

CLOGS—Holland

I think our ballerinas in the Soviet Union
are the best in the world.
Someday I will be one, too.
At first it hurt to stand on my toes,
even though the tips of my ballet shoes
are stiff and padded.
But I practice every day.
Now I can twirl across the stage.
My toe shoes lift me high into the air.
I am a graceful, flying swan!

18

BALLET SHOES—The Soviet Union

In Lapland, our boots are made from reindeer hide.
Their pointed toes curl up at the end.
Sometimes we stuff our boots
with moss or sedge grass
to make them warmer.

REINDEER BOOTS—Lapland

It is hot in Mexico,

so we don't need much of a shoe.

We go barefoot or wear sandals.

My sandals protect the bottom of my feet

from rocks and mud,

but they let the breeze cool my toes.

These woven leather sandals

are called huaraches (wah-RAH-cheese).

As soon as I find my huaraches,

my mother and I will go to the market.

HUARACHES—Mexico